MYRIAD BOOKS LIMITED
35 Bishopsthorpe Road, London SE26 4PA

First published by
Andersen Press
20 Vauxhall Bridge Road
London SW1V 2SA
www.andersenpress.co.uk

ISBN 1 904 736 81 5

Printed in China

THE
SCARECROW'S HAT

Written and illustrated by
Ken Brown

Myriad Books

"That's a nice hat," said Chicken to the scarecrow.

"Yes, it is," replied the scarecrow, "but I'd rather have a walking stick. I've been standing here for years and my arms are so tired. I'd love a walking stick to lean on. I'd swap my hat for a walking stick any day."

Now Chicken didn't have a walking stick, but she knew someone who did.

"That's a nice walking stick," said Chicken to the badger.

"Yes, it is," replied the badger, "but I'd rather have a piece of ribbon.
It gets hot and stuffy underground so I prop my door open with my stick,
but I'm always tripping over it. If I had a ribbon I could *tie* the door open.
I'd swap my walking stick for a ribbon any day."

Now Chicken didn't have a ribbon,
but she knew someone who did.

"That's a nice ribbon," said Chicken to the jackdaw.

"Yes, it is," said the jackdaw," but I'd rather have some wool. My nest is on this high, stone ledge and it's very hard to sit on. I'd love some warm, soft wool to line it with. I'd swap this ribbon for some wool any day."

Now Chicken didn't have any wool, but she knew someone who did.

"That's a nice wool coat," said Chicken to the sheep.

"Yes, it is," replied the sheep, "but I'd rather have a pair of glasses. I have to keep a look out for the wolf and my eyes are not as good as they used to be. I really need a pair of glasses. I'd swap some of my wool for a pair of glasses any day."

Now Chicken didn't have a pair of glasses, but she knew someone who did.

"That's a nice pair of glasses," said Chicken to the owl.

"Yes, it is," replied the owl. "My old ones broke, so I had to get a new pair. But I'd rather have a blanket. The sun streams through my window and keeps me awake all day, which wouldn't matter if I had a good thick blanket to sleep under. I'd swap my glasses for a blanket any day."

Now Chicken didn't have a blanket,
but she knew someone who did.

"That's a nice blanket," said Chicken to the donkey.

"Yes, it is," replied the donkey, "But I'd rather have a few feathers. The flies drive me mad, buzzing round my ears. My tail isn't quite long enough to flick them away, but if I had some long feathers tied to the end of it, I could swat them easily. I'd swap my blanket for a few long feathers any day.

Quick as a flash, Chicken pulled out one, two, three of her longest feathers and tied them to the donkey's tail.

The donkey was delighted and, true to his word, swapped his blanket
for the feathers.

Chicken took the blanket to the owl —
who swapped it for his glasses (the old ones, of course).

She took the glasses to the sheep —
who swapped them for her wool.

She took the wool to the jackdaw —
who swapped it for her ribbon.

She took the ribbon to the badger —
who swapped it for his walking stick.

Finally, she took the walking stick to the scarecrow.
With a grateful sigh of relief, he leant his tired old arms on the stick
and gladly swapped it for his battered old hat.
Chicken took the hat and filled it with fresh, sweet-smelling straw. . .

"That's a nice nest," said the duck.
"Yes, it is," replied Chicken, "and I wouldn't swap it for *anything!*"